Not Again!

An Ivy and Mack story

Contents

Written by Jane Clarke

Illustrated by Gustavo Mazali

with Nadene Naude

Collins

What's in this story?

Listen and say

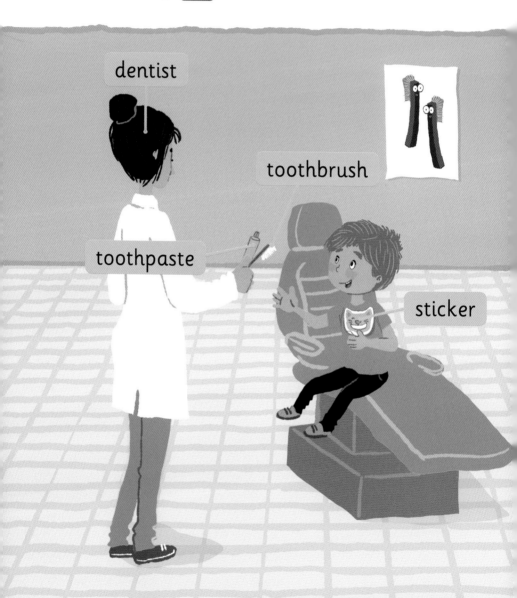

dentist

toothbrush

toothpaste

sticker

Download the audio at www.collins.co.uk/839752

FLOSS

Chapter 1 I don't want to go to the dentist

Mum and Dad were **busy**. Mack and Ivy were busy, too. They had lots of stickers.

"Give me the **drill**, please," said Mum.

My tooth hurts!

Ivy put a sticker on her face. "OW!" she said. "My tooth hurts!"

"Is it a baby tooth?" asked Mack.

"No!" said Ivy. "Don't tell Mum and Dad. I don't want to go to the dentist!"

"But the dentist has great stickers!" said Mack.

"This crocodile sticker's no good now," said Mack, "I need a new one and only the dentist has them!"

"Well, I don't want to go to the dentist," Ivy told him.

"OW!" said Dad.

"Are you hurt?" asked Mum.

"The **coffee** is hot," said Dad.

Ivy's biscuit had **nuts** and **seeds** in it.
Her tooth hurt but she did not tell Mum.

It's my tooth!

OW!

Chapter 2 My tooth hurts!

In the afternoon, Mack and Ivy played football and ate ice cream.

"Do you have **toothache** again?" asked Mack.

Mack's tooth did not hurt, but he wanted to go to the dentist and get a new sticker.

"OWWW! My tooth!" he said.

"What's the matter?" Mum and Dad asked.

"I need to go to the dentist!" said Mack.

Mum looked in his mouth. "No, you don't. Your teeth are OK, Mack," she said.

Ivy could not eat her pizza.

"What's the matter?" asked Mum.

"My tooth hurts," said Ivy.

"Toothache isn't nice," said Dad.

"You need to go to the dentist," Mum told Ivy.
"We can all go."

"I don't need the dentist," said Ivy. "I only need to clean my teeth!"

"Good idea!" said Dad.

"I need to clean my teeth AND go to the dentist," Mack said.

Ivy, Mack and Dad cleaned their teeth.

"Does your tooth hurt?" Dad asked Ivy.

"Yes, it does," Ivy said.

"My tooth hurts, too, sometimes," said Dad.

Mum said, "I spoke to the dentist and we can go on Saturday."

"Great!" said Mack.

"Oh no!" said Ivy.

"I'm busy on Saturday!" said Dad.

"You're not busy on Saturday," Mum told Dad.

Chapter 3 What do dentists do?

On Saturday, Mum said, "Let's go to the dentist!"

"I **really** don't want to go," Ivy said.

"Why not?" asked Mack.

"Dentists use a drill to fix your tooth!"
Ivy told Mack.

Mack thought of the dentist with a **huge** drill.

"I'm very sorry you have a bad tooth, Ivy,"
Mack said.

"So am I," said Ivy.

"Don't be afraid," said Mum. "The dentist takes out the bad part of a tooth. Then, he fixes it and then ... it doesn't hurt!"

"Ivy's right!" said Mack. "We don't want to go to the dentist!"

"Dentists help us!" Mum said. She looked at Dad. "Don't they?"

"They do!" said Dad. "We are *not* afraid! We can do this. Come on!"

Chapter 4 The dentist is ready for you!

"The dentist is **ready**," said the nurse.
"Who's **first**?"

Mum went into the room with the nurse.

Not me!

"The dentist needs to fix your bad tooth, Dad!" said Mack.

"I know," said Dad.

Mum came out. "All good!" She smiled. "Come on, Mack. You're next!"

Mack sat in the dentist's chair.
"Open your mouth!" said the dentist.

The dentist **carefully** looked at each tooth.

"Well done, Mack," he said. "You have very
nice teeth! I can see you clean them every day."

"I do!" said Mack. "Can I have
a crocodile sticker?"

The dentist gave Mack a new toothbrush, some toothpaste and lots of stickers.

"I like the dentist!" said Mack. "Now you, Ivy!"

"Dad can go next," said Ivy.

"OK, Ivy." said Dad.

When Dad came out, he smiled. "My tooth needed a **filling**, but it didn't hurt at all!"

"See, Ivy? The dentist fixed Dad's tooth. Now you go in!" said Mack.

"I don't want to go in there!" said Ivy.

"You can do this, Ivy!" Dad told her.

Chapter 5 Not again, Ivy!

Ivy sat in the dentist's big chair.

"Open your mouth!" The dentist looked carefully at each tooth.

"I can see what's hurting your teeth," he said. "There's a seed between two of them. Let me take it out!"

"You fixed it!" Ivy smiled. "Thank you!" Ivy was very happy.

The dentist gave Ivy a toothbrush and toothpaste. "Would you like some stickers, too?"

When they got home, Mack played dentists with Croc.

Ivy and Dad made their favourite biscuits.

"These biscuits have got nuts and seeds in them," Dad said. "Be careful, Ivy!"

Ivy took a biscuit. "My favourite biscuits," she said. "OW!"

"Oh no! Not again, Ivy!" said Mum, Dad and Mack.

Ivy smiled. "The biscuit is hot but my teeth are fine!"

Mack laughed and gave everyone a sticker.

Mini-dictionary

Listen and read

busy (adjective) Someone who is **busy** is doing lots of things, and has no time to do anything else.

carefully (adverb) If you do something **carefully**, you take time and do it as well as you can.

coffee (noun) **Coffee** is a hot drink. You make it from the beans of the coffee plant.

drill (noun) A **drill** is a tool that you use to make holes.

filling (noun) A **filling** is something that the dentist puts into a hole in a tooth, to fix it.

first (adjective) Someone who is **first** comes before everyone else.

huge (adjective) Something that is **huge** is very big.

nut (noun) A **nut** is a dry fruit with a hard shell.

ready (adjective) If someone is **ready**, they can do something now.

really (adverb) You use **really** to show how much you want to do something.

seed (noun) A **seed** is the small hard part of a plant that can grow into a new plant.

toothache (noun) **Toothache** is when one of your teeth hurts.

1 Look and order the story

2 Listen and say

Collins

Published by Collins
An imprint of HarperCollins*Publishers*
Westerhill Road
Bishopbriggs
Glasgow
G64 2QT

HarperCollins*Publishers*
1st Floor, Watermarque Building
Ringsend Road
Dublin 4
Ireland

William Collins' dream of knowledge for all began with the publication of his first book in 1819.

A self-educated mill worker, he not only enriched millions of lives, but also founded a flourishing publishing house. Today, staying true to this spirit, Collins books are packed with inspiration, innovation and practical expertise. They place you at the centre of a world of possibility and give you exactly what you need to explore it.

© HarperCollins*Publishers* Limited 2020

10 9 8 7 6 5 4 3 2

ISBN 978-0-00-839752-4

www.collins.co.uk/elt

British Library Cataloguing in Publication Data

A catalogue record for this publication is available from the British Library.

Author: Jane Clarke
Lead illustrator: Gustavo Mazali (Beehive)
Copy illustrator: Nadene Naude (Beehive)
Series editor: Rebecca Adlard
Publishing manager: Lisa Todd
Product managers: Jennifer Hall and Caroline Green
In-house editor: Alma Puts Keren
Project manager: Emily Hooton
Editor: Deborah Friedland
Proofreaders: Natalie Murray and Michael Lamb
Cover designer: Kevin Robbins
Typesetter: 2Hoots Publishing Services Ltd
Audio produced by id audio, London
Reading guide author: Julie Penn
Production controller: Rachel Weaver
Printed and bound by: GPS Group, Slovenia

Download the audio for this book and a reading guide for parents and teachers at www.collins.co.uk/839752